THE CLUMPETS GO SAILING

Story by Jan Wahl *Illustrated by* Cyndy Szekeres

Parents' Magazine Press
New York

Printed in the United States of America

Library of Congress Cataloging in Publications Data
Wahl, Jan.
The Clumpets go sailing.
SUMMARY: The Clumpet family sails to a sick uncle's house to take him some hot soup.
I. Szekeres, Cyndy, illus. II. Title.
PZ7.W1266Cl [E] 73-23083
ISBN 0-8193-0770-X ISBN 0-8193-0771-8 (lib. bdg.)

for Else from Lorenzo

Mr. Clumpet's brother, Uncle Skinny, was sick.
A robin brought the message, dropping it down the Clumpets' chimney.

“A message from out of the sky!” cried several voices.
Mrs. Clumpet stopped washing lettuce.
Mr. Clumpet read the message.

"We must take poor Skinny some hot soup!"
Mrs. Clumpet was the best soup-maker around.
She brought out her biggest pot.

Mr. Clumpet put on his captain's hat.
Then he said, "We will go to Skinny's by boat.
That way the soup will not spill."

The children, Arthur and Emily, were delighted.
This meant they did not have to go to school.
They decided to take Uncle Skinny a few toys.

"But Mr. Clumpet," declared his wife Lizzie, "we have no boat!"
However, Mr. Clumpet was already taking off the front door.
It would make a splendid boat.
Arthur and Emily helped carry the door-boat down to the stream.
The stream went straight through the forest to Uncle Skinny's house.

The door-boat sat upon the water, floating nicely.
But the current wasn't strong enough; the boat wouldn't budge.
"Whatever shall we do?" asked Mrs. Clumpet, fretting.
"Please get the tablecloth," Mr. Clumpet said.
"And bring the vacuum cleaner, too, Lizzie."

"Herman, what are you going to clean?" his wife asked.

But as soon as she had brought them, Mr. Clumpet and the children fastened the vacuum cleaner to the boat.
The handle made a mast, and the tablecloth a gay sail.
The motor, of course, made a motor.

Alas, the vacuum cleaner was so heavy the boat began to sink.
Emily, the sail trimmer, teetered. Mr. Clumpet took off the machine.
Mrs. Clumpet was happy, for she had been wondering where
they would plug it in. She offered the hall hat rack instead.
It made a sturdy mast.
The steaming soup pot was put aboard.
Emily and Arthur helped stir the hot, thick soup.

TOOOLZ

Then, at last, a wind came up. "CAST OFF!" cried Mr. Clumpet. Using a broom to push them from shore, they set sail. *Swish, swish, swish.* Everybody helped.

The voyagers were greeted by friends who sat around enjoying the afternoon.

"There go the Clumpets sailing!" they said in admiration.

Through the tiny window in the door, the Clumpets watched the fish at the bottom of the stream.
The fish looked up at them.

The soup smelled so delicious that bees and butterflies
buzzed and flittered. The Clumpets shooed them away.
Mrs. Clumpet's hat blew off the mast and into the water.
A green bullfrog brought it back in his mouth, swimming briskly.
Mrs. Clumpet was very grateful.

PORTUG
ANCHOVIS
TENIR AU FRAIS

At his house downstream lay poor feverish Uncle Skinny.
His head was propped on many pillows, a cold cloth resting on his snout.

"Can't you go faster, dear?" asked Mrs. Clumpet.
"The soup is getting cold."
Quickly Mr. Clumpet paddled with the broom.
But he soon tired of this and let the boat drift along
while he played cards with Mrs. Clumpet.

Now the current was beginning to run.
Arthur and Emily watched their toy boats bobbing behind on strings.
Their eyes felt droopy. The next thing they knew...

The big sun was setting behind them.
The children curled up together.
Mrs. Clumpet quietly sang a song.
Mr. Clumpet had brought a lantern, which he now lit.
The whole dark night through he stood watch, steering.

Finally, he too grew tired.
All the Clumpets were fast asleep.
Their boat drifted right past Uncle Skinny's!

Luckily, Uncle Skinny was feeling better.
He happened to look out the window.

He rushed out with a long pole—just in time to save them from tumbling over the rapids.

The Clumpets woke up.
Mr. and Mrs! Emily and Arthur!
They were so happy to see Uncle Skinny.
They were so happy they hadn't gone over the roaring rapids.

They went inside and heated the soup
because it had grown cold.
The Clumpets were so hungry they could have finished all the soup
themselves.
But they remembered why they had come.

And Uncle Skinny got lots, too.
He certainly deserved it!